Playground Day!

by Jennifer J. Merz

Clarion Books   New York

Clarion Books
a Houghton Mifflin Company imprint
215 Park Avenue South, New York, NY 10003
Copyright © 2007 by Jennifer J. Merz

The illustrations were executed in cut and torn paper. The text was set in 28-point Lomba Book.

www.clarionbooks.com

Printed in Singapore

Library of Congress Cataloging-in-Publication Data
Merz, Jennifer J.
Playground day / by Jennifer J. Merz
p. cm.
Summary: Children play on the playground, imitating
animals from bunnies and squirrels to elephants and penguins.
ISBN: 978-0-618-81696-5
[1. Playgrounds—Fiction. 2. Play—Fiction. 3. Animals—Fiction. 4. Stories in rhyme.] I. Title.
PZ8.3.M55923 Pl 2007
[E] 22
2006039215

ISBN-13: 978-0-618-81696-5
ISBN-10: 0-618-81696-8

TWP 10 9 8 7 6 5 4 3 2 1

To Lesley and Julia
and all those wonderful playground days

Sunny smiles,
pretend and play.
Hurray, hurray!
It's playground day!

Skipping, giggling,
springing, wiggling,

I hop like a . . .

BUNNY

Scurry, scatter,
chitter, chatter,

I hide like a . . .

SQUIRREL

Stretching, swaying,
jungle playing,

I climb like a . . .

MONKEY

Breezes blow.
Up I go!

I fly like a . . .

BIRD

Running, racing,
riding, chasing,

I gallop like a . . .

HORSE

Tilting, tipping,
gliding, slipping,

I slide like a . . .

PENGUIN

Water quenches.
Fountain drenches!

I spray like an . . .

ELEPHANT

Bouncing, bumping,
crouching, jumping,

I leap like a . . .

FROG

Digging, mixing,
pouring, fixing,

I build like a . . .

BEAVER

Crispy crunching,
snacktime munching,

I nibble like a . . .

MOUSE

The playground's
so much fun today.
I run, I play . . . I want to stay!

Sun is setting, moon's in sight.
Let's head home before it's night.

Pick up, pack up,
put away . . .

We'll be back another day.